ER 1B

Knock, knock. Who's there?

Nancy was really looking forward to April's party.

They soon reached the Funks' house. There were no cars in the driveway. The curtains in all the windows were closed.

"It looks like nobody's home," Nancy observed.

"No way." Bess marched up to the front door and knocked. "Hello?"

A moment passed. No one answered.

Bess was about to knock again when Nancy noticed something. The door was open a crack.

Nancy stepped forward and pushed the door open slightly. It made a creaking noise. She gulped.

All of a sudden the screeching sound of sirens w̲_____ ars. A voice called ou_____ g on private property._____ t!"

D1010310

Join the CLUE CREW
& solve these other cases!

NANCY DREW

AND THE CLUE CREW®

#19

April Fool's Day

BY CAROLYN KEENE

ILLUSTRATED BY MACKY PAMINTUAN

Aladdin Paperbacks
New York London Toronto Sydney

❧ ALADDIN PAPERBACKS

An imprint of Simon & Schuster Children's Publishing Division

1230 Avenue of the Americas, New York, NY 10020

Text copyright © 2009 by Simon & Schuster, Inc.

Illustrations copyright © 2009 by Macky Pamintuan

All rights reserved, including the right of reproduction in whole or in part in any form.

NANCY DREW, NANCY DREW AND THE CLUE CREW, ALADDIN PAPERBACKS, and related logo are registered trademarks of Simon & Schuster, Inc.

Designed by Lisa Vega

The text of this book was set in ITC Stone Informal.

Manufactured in the United States of America

First Aladdin Paperbacks edition March 2009

10 9 8 7 6 5 4 3 2 1

Library of Congress Control Number 2008928034

ISBN-13: 978-1-4169-7518-2

ISBN-10: 1-4169-7518-7

CONTENTS

CHAPTER ONE

A Mysterious Invitation

"You got a letter, Nancy," Hannah Gruen said.

Eight-year-old Nancy Drew glanced up from her blueberry bagel with extra cream cheese. Hannah was on the other side of the kitchen counter, sorting through the day's mail.

"Who's it from?" Nancy asked curiously.

"I'm not sure, honey," replied Hannah.

She handed Nancy a plain white envelope. Nancy licked the cream cheese from her fingers before taking the envelope and studying it carefully. Her name and address were typed on the front. There was a River Heights postmark and a stamp with a picture of spring flowers. There was no return address.

"Hmm, it's a mystery," Nancy said thoughtfully.

Hannah chuckled. She knew how much Nancy loved mysteries. Nancy and her two best friends, George Fayne and Bess Marvin, had started their own detective club called the Clue Crew. They solved all sorts of cases—everything from catching an escaped pony to finding missing baby chicks.

Hannah was the Drews' housekeeper. But she was much more than that. She had lived with Nancy and her father, Carson Drew, since Nancy's mother had died five years ago.

Nancy picked up a letter opener and slit open the envelope. Inside was an official-looking card. Across the front of the card, it said:

REPORT CARD
GRADING PERIOD:
  SPRING
STUDENT:
  NANCY DREW

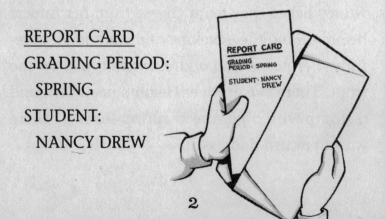

Nancy gulped. Her report card? She wasn't sure she wanted to see that right now. The math test last Friday had been superhard. And what if her teacher, Mrs. Ramirez, hadn't liked her essay on the rain forest?

"What is it, Nancy?" Hannah asked her.

"It's, uh, my report card," Nancy replied nervously.

"Your report card!" Hannah exclaimed. "Isn't it a little early for that?"

Nancy shrugged. She took a deep breath, opened it—and gasped.

Inside, there were no As—or Bs, or Cs, or Ds. There were no comments from Mrs. Ramirez. Instead there was an announcement in big bold letters:

APRIL FOOL'S DAY!
WELL, NOT JUST YET.
I'M HAVING AN APRIL FOOL'S DAY PARTY, AND YOU'RE INVITED!
THERE WILL BE LOTS OF FOOD AND GAMES.

MAKE SURE TO BRING A GAG,
BECAUSE THERE WILL BE A GRAND PRIZE
FOR THE BEST ONE!

Nancy read the rest of the invitation. It was from April Funk, who lived down the street. April had moved to River Heights a few months ago. Like Nancy, she was in third grade at River Heights Elementary School, although she was in a different class.

Nancy, George, and Bess had quickly become friends with April, who had a great sense of humor. April was always telling jokes and pulling goofy pranks. It was just like her to throw an April Fool's Day party, and to send such a funny invitation, too!

"Well, that's a lot better than a report card, isn't it?" Hannah laughed as she read the invitation over Nancy's shoulder.

"Definitely," Nancy agreed.

The phone rang just then. Hannah picked it

up. "Hello?" she said. "Oh, hi, Bess. Yes, she's sitting right here." Hannah handed the phone to Nancy. "For you."

Nancy grabbed the phone. "Hi, Bess!"

"Hi, Nancy," Bess said. "Did you, uh, just get your report card?"

Nancy giggled. "I just got it. Did you, uh, just get your report card too?"

"Yup, and so did George," Bess replied. "Yay! We're all going to April's party! Oh my gosh, I have to start figuring out what to wear!"

Bess and George were cousins. But they were more different than alike. Bess was really into fashion. George's passion was computers.

"And we have to start figuring out what to bring," Nancy reminded her. "Did you see what the invitation said? We all have to bring a gag."

"Oh, right," said Bess. "Where will we get one?"

"I know where we can get some cool gags,"

Nancy said. "What are you and George doing tomorrow after school?"

"This is the funnest store I've ever been to!" Bess exclaimed.

"Me too," George piped up.

"Me three," Nancy chimed in.

The three girls were walking around Gagtime, accompanied by Hannah. Gagtime was a new store in downtown River Heights. Nancy had seen an ad for the store in the *River Heights Bugle.* Its motto was: "Your one-stop shopping for gags, pranks, and practical jokes."

Nancy couldn't believe all the things in the store: blue, purple, and orange wigs; sunglasses that made your eyes look big and crazy; chattering teeth and skulls; tubes of lip gloss with fake spiders in them; calculators that squirted water at you when you pressed the equals sign. There were even bags of candy that turned your mouth black, bars of white soap that turned your hands red, and fortune cookies with silly sayings inside. And there were dozens and dozens of other goofy items too.

"How are you girls going to decide what to buy?" Hannah asked them.

"I want to buy one of everything!" Bess said. She glanced inside her puffy pink purse. "Except . . . I only have four dollars and eighty-three cents."

"It's going to be hard to choose," Nancy said.

"Well, let me know if you need any help," said Hannah. "I'll be right over there in the joke book section."

"Okay, Hannah," Nancy said. She turned to her friends. "Let's shop!"

George picked up the calculator. "I kind of like this. I can squirt April!"

"This is going to be the best party ever," Bess said excitedly. "If anyone's going to throw a really awesome April Fool's Day party, it's April Funk!"

Just then Nancy saw someone out of the

corner of her eye. It was a girl, and she seemed to be eavesdropping on their conversation. She was standing a few feet away, behind a display of fake desserts.

The girl stepped forward. "April Funk's party? What are you talking about?" she demanded in an angry voice.

ChAPTER TWO

An Unwelcome Welcome

Nancy stared at the girl. She had short black hair and cool-looking glasses—and a big frown on her face.

Nancy recognized her. It was Sydney Decker from school. Sydney was supersmart; she'd won first place in the science fair last week.

"Uh, hi, Sydney," Nancy said. She wasn't sure why Sydney seemed so upset.

Sydney narrowed her eyes. "Don't try to change the subject, Nancy Drew," she huffed. "I want you to tell me everything you know about this so-called party—right this second!"

Nancy, George, and Bess all looked at one another. Bess frowned as if to say, *What's up with*

Sydney? George shrugged, meaning, *Who knows?*

"Why do you want to know about April's party?" Nancy asked Sydney curiously.

Sydney ignored her question. "You're talking about *the* April Funk, right? April Funk who's in my class at River Heights Elementary School? The one with the curly red hair? The one with the purple backpack? The one whose favorite food is chocolate-covered pretzels?"

"Yes, *that* April Funk," George piped up. "Except I didn't know her favorite food was chocolate-covered pretzels."

"Ha!" Sydney scoffed. "So where is this party taking place? And when?"

"It's at her house, four o'clock, April Fool's Day," Bess replied.

"We're here because the invitation said there's going to be a grand prize for the best gag," added Nancy.

"Hmm, interesting," Sydney said. "Who else is invited, besides the three of you?"

"How would we know that?" said George.

"Sydney, why are you asking us all these questions?" Nancy asked impatiently.

Nancy thought she saw a flicker of hurt in Sydney's eyes. "Well, if you must know, April happens to be my BFF," Sydney replied after a moment. "And as her BFF, I think I'm entitled to this information. Don't you?"

"Oh!" Nancy exclaimed.

Just then a teenage girl came rushing up to Sydney. She had a lime green cell phone glued to one ear. "Syd, we gotta go, we're gonna be late for your cello lesson," she said. "Come on, come on!"

"I am *way* too mature to need a babysitter," Sydney grumbled to Nancy and her friends. "Bye. See you in school, I guess."

"Bye," the three girls said in unison.

"And you'd better not repeat a word of this conversation to April," Sydney warned.

With that, she turned on her heel and left.

"I guess April didn't invite Sydney to her party," Nancy said.

"Yeah, otherwise Sydney wouldn't have been asking us for all the details," George agreed.

"But she said she's April's BFF. So why wouldn't April invite her?" Bess wondered.

Nancy and her friends were walking to April's party. It was a beautiful spring afternoon. Tulips, daffodils, and hyacinths swayed in the warm breeze as they made their way to April's house, which was just down the block from where Nancy lived.

The girls were carrying their gags from Gagtime in their backpacks. Nancy had bought the fortune cookies with the silly sayings inside. George got the calculator that squirted water. And Bess purchased the lip gloss with the fake spider in it.

Nancy was really looking forward to April's party. Still, she wished she knew what was going on with Sydney and April. It was kind of a mystery.

They soon reached the Funks' house. It was a big Victorian house painted in different shades of purple. The front porch was cluttered with toys.

Nancy glanced around—and frowned. There were no cars in the driveway. The curtains in all the windows were closed.

"It looks like nobody's home," Nancy observed.

"No way." Bess marched up to the front door and knocked. "Hello?"

A moment passed. No one answered.

"Hello?" Bess repeated.

Still no one answered.

"This is weird," George whispered.

"Did we get the date wrong or something?" Bess asked Nancy.

Nancy reached into her backpack and pulled out her invitation. "It says April first, four p.m. Today is April first."

George held up her wrist and pointed to her watch. "And it's exactly four o'clock right now."

"Okay, then, we're definitely supposed to be here," said Bess.

Bess was about to knock again when Nancy noticed something. The door was open a crack.

Nancy stepped forward and pushed the door open slightly. It made a creaking noise. She gulped.

"What are you doing, Nancy?" Bess hissed.

14

Nancy poked her head in. "Hello? Is anyone home?" she said loudly.

All of a sudden the screeching sound of sirens was blaring in their ears. A voice called out, "You are trespassing on private property. You are all under arrest!"

ChAPTER THREE

The Unexpected Guest

The sirens continued screeching.

"It's the police!" George cried out.

"Omigosh, are we in trouble?" said Bess frantically.

Nancy covered her ears. The sirens were really loud.

She started to say, "Let's get out of here!" But it was too late. Before she could get the words out of her mouth, the door swung wide open.

Nancy gasped. The person standing on the other side was not a police officer. It was April! She was holding a toy siren in one hand and a megaphone in the other. She was dressed in jeans and a yellow T-shirt with a clown face on it.

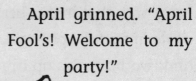

April grinned. "April Fool's! Welcome to my party!"

"April, that was *you*?" Nancy exclaimed.

"You scared us!" Bess added.

"You should give *yourself* the grand prize for the best gag," George told April.

"I totally should, shouldn't I?" April waved the girls inside. "Come on in! Everyone's down in the basement."

Nancy, George, and Bess followed April into the house. They were immediately greeted by a big calico cat and a smaller black-and-white cat. The cats rubbed up against the girls' ankles, meowing and purring.

"The big one's Mr. Tuna. And the other one's Lipstick, because she has that white mark around

17

her mouth that makes her look like she's wearing white lipstick," April said. "Plus, I have a bunny and two hamsters up in my room. The bunny's name is Carrots, and the hamsters' names are Fuzzy and Wuzzy."

Nancy, George, and Bess giggled at the funny names. "It's cool that you have so many pets," Nancy said.

April's house was big and sprawling. The rooms were painted bright, fun colors like lemon yellow and lime green and turquoise. Kids' artwork was plastered all over the walls.

April's parents were in the kitchen preparing snacks. Mr. Funk had a big bushy beard and mustache. Mrs. Funk had curly red hair like April. April introduced the three girls to them.

"Welcome, ladies!" Mrs. Funk said. "I'd shake your hands, but mine are covered in chocolate frosting."

Bess's eyes lit up. "Yum, chocolate frosting! I hope we're having cupcakes."

Mrs. Funk smiled mysteriously. "Maybe. Maybe not."

"I hope April's little joke didn't scare you girls too much," said Mr. Funk.

"Well, it did, but it was pretty funny, too," George replied.

"Nancy! George! Bess! Come on, everyone's waiting downstairs," April said eagerly.

The three girls said good-bye to Mr. and Mrs. Funk and trailed downstairs after April. When they reached the basement rec room, Nancy started cracking up. The room had been decorated wall-to-wall with an April Fool's Day theme. There were fake spilled drinks, chattering teeth, and handmade posters filled with jokes and riddles, like:

What did the banana say to the doctor?
"I'm not peeling well."

Two girls were sitting on a faded brown leather couch. A third girl was checking out the posters. The two girls on the couch looked very similar. They both had straight, shoulder-length blond hair with bangs. They were both wearing jean skirts and hot pink tops. When they smiled, Nancy could see that they both had hot pink braces.

April introduced them as her friends Miranda and Heidi.

"Are you sisters?" Bess asked them.

Miranda frowned. "Uh, no. Why would you think *that*?"

Bess turned to Nancy and George. "Maybe because they have identical hair and outfits?" she whispered.

"Miranda and Heidi go to my old school," April explained. She pointed to the girl who was checking out the posters. "So does Katie."

"Hi!" Katie called out in a friendly voice. She wore her brown hair in a ponytail, and she was dressed in a red soccer jersey and jeans.

"Do you play soccer?" George asked her.

Katie nodded. "I *love* soccer! It's my favorite sport in the whole world."

"Mine too," George said.

Heidi rolled her eyes. "Soccer is *soooo* boring. Soccermania is way more interesting." She reached into her backpack and pulled out a small flower-covered device. It had a shiny screen and lots of tiny buttons.

"What's that?" Nancy asked.

"What? You mean you don't know?" said Miranda. "It's only the coolest gaming console ever."

"It's the new Gamer Girl," Heidi explained. "You can play Soccermania and a bunch of other games on it. You can't get it in the United States yet. Daddy bought it for me in Japan, on a business trip." She added, "It cost a *lot* of money."

"So did this." Miranda reached into her backpack and pulled out a small red cell phone. "It's the new My-Fone. You can't get this in the United States either. Mommy bought it for me in Sweden."

George leaned over to Nancy and Bess. "Miranda's in third grade and she's allowed to have a cell phone?" she said with a gasp.

"I bet none of *you* have the new Gamer Girl or the new My-Fone," Heidi said smugly.

"Uh, Heidi? And Miranda? It's not cool to brag," Katie pointed out. "You're probably making everyone here feel bad."

Miranda sighed. "We're not bragging, Katie. We're just stating the facts—right, H?"

Heidi tossed her blond hair over her shoulders. "Right, M."

Nancy noticed that April was staring at Miranda and Heidi with a puzzled expression. Nancy was puzzled too. She wondered why April was friends with them. Based on a first impression, they seemed kind of stuck-up. And April was definitely *not* stuck-up.

April turned to the rest of the girls. "Uh, maybe we should play a game or something," she said awkwardly.

Just then the doorbell rang.

"More party guests, April?" Miranda asked.

"No. Everyone's already here," said April, confused.

From upstairs came the sound of the door opening . . . then voices . . . then footsteps. A moment later someone came down the basement stairs.

It was Sydney Decker!

ChaPTER FOUR

Missing!

"I'm sorry I'm late, April," Sydney said with an apologetic smile. "I hope I didn't miss anything."

"M-miss anything?" April stammered. "W-what are you talking about?"

Nancy noticed that April looked really uncomfortable. *No wonder*, she thought. She hadn't invited Sydney to the party—and Sydney had shown up anyway!

"I guess my invitation must have gotten lost in the mail," Sydney breezed on. She set her backpack on the floor, next to everyone else's. It was bright blue, with dolphin stickers on it. "It's a good thing I ran into Nancy, George, and Bess at Gagtime. They told me all about the party and invited me. Wasn't that nice of them?"

"What?" Nancy, George, and Bess said at the same time.

"I brought some chocolate chip cookies for everyone to share." Sydney held up a pan covered with aluminum foil. "I baked them this morning from a recipe that I found online. Where should I put them?"

April hesitated. "Um, over on that table," she said after a moment, pointing. "Thanks, Sydney. That was nice of you."

"You're welcome!" said Sydney. "So are you going to introduce me to your other friends?"

April introduced Sydney to Miranda, Heidi, and Katie. Miranda barely said hello; she was talking to someone on her cell phone. Likewise, Heidi was furiously pressing the buttons on her Gamer Girl.

Bess pulled Nancy and George away from the others. "Sydney told a big fat lie!" she said in a low voice.

"We did *not* invite her to April's party," George agreed.

"She must have really, really wanted to come to the party," Nancy mused. "I wonder if she and April are really BFFs, or if that's a big fat lie too."

"It probably is, since April didn't invite her to the party," Bess pointed out.

"Who's hungry?"

Nancy glanced up. Mr. and Mrs. Funk were coming down the stairs with trays of snacks.

April's face lit up. "Oh, awesome! Thanks, Mom and Dad. Hey, everyone! Wait till you check out these superspecial party snacks that we made."

Mr. and Mrs. Funk set the food down on a large table surrounded by eight red folding chairs. April, Nancy, George, Bess, Sydney, and Katie gathered around. Miranda put her cell phone back in her backpack and joined the others. Heidi did likewise with her Gamer Girl.

"Eeeew!" April's friends all cried out at once.

On one of the trays was a kitty litter pan full of kitty litter—and kitty poops! It was sitting on some old newspapers, and there was a shiny new pooper scooper sticking out of it.

"That is *soooo* disgusting!" Heidi moaned.

"Really gross," Miranda agreed.

April started laughing. So did her parents.

Sydney frowned. "What's so amusing about kitty litter? What if some of us had eaten it by accident? We might have gotten sick—or worse!"

"April Fool's!" April exclaimed. "It's not really kitty litter."

"It's not? Then what is it?" asked Nancy.

"It's a special recipe made of cake and cookie crumbs mixed with chocolate pudding and frosting," Mr. Funk explained.

Bess made a face. "And what are the . . . um . . . little things made of?"

"We microwaved some caramel candies until they were soft and rolled them into kitty poop shapes," April told her guests.

Everyone cracked up. Nancy had to admit that this was a really good April Fool's Day prank!

Katie glanced at the other items on the table. "Well, at least there's some *real* food here. Hey, french fries—my favorite!" She grabbed a french fry out of a basket and dipped it into a small

dish of ketchup. She popped it into her mouth—
and almost spit it out. "This isn't a french fry.
It's sweet!"

"It's baked bread dough rolled in sugar. And
the 'ketchup' is strawberry jam," Mrs. Funk
explained.

George studied the remaining snacks. "Is the

other stuff April Fool's Day food too?" she asked hesitantly.

April grinned. "Maybe. See for yourself!"

"Don't worry, it's all edible," Mr. Funk reassured the girls. "Enjoy!" With that, he and Mrs. Funk went back upstairs.

"I'm going to wash my hands first," Katie said. "I got ketchup—I mean, strawberry jam—on them. I'll be right back." She rushed to the bathroom, which was in the far corner of the basement.

Nancy and the others sat down at the table and helped themselves to the snacks. Katie rejoined them a few minutes later and dug in too. There were "green beans" made of rolled green fruit candy that had been microwaved and reshaped. There were apples with holes in them and gummy worms sticking out of the holes. And to drink there was "Martian milk," which was milk with green food coloring in it.

They also ate the chocolate chip cookies that

Sydney had brought. They were just regular old chocolate chip cookies, and they were delicious.

April smiled at everyone around the table. "So . . . what kind of gags did you all bring? Let's check them out!"

"Let's!" Bess said eagerly.

Nancy, George, Bess, Sydney, and Katie all got up from the table and went over to their backpacks. They got their gags and brought them back to the table. Miranda and Heidi stayed where they were.

Nancy passed out her fortune cookies with goofy sayings in them. April broke her cookie in half and read her message out loud. "Mine says, 'Help! I'm being held prisoner in a fortune cookie factory.' Ha-ha!"

Bess grossed everyone out with her lip gloss with the spider in it. George tricked April with her squirting calculator. And Sydney shared her bag of candy that made your mouth turn black. Nancy remembered seeing it at Gagtime.

Katie had brought an egg carton to which

she'd glued all the eggs inside. "I made another one at home this morning," she explained. "I put it in the refrigerator, and when my dad tried to make eggs, they broke and gushed all over his hands!"

"What about you guys?" April asked Miranda and Heidi. "What did you bring?"

Miranda and Heidi exchanged a glance. "We, uh, kind of forgot to bring anything," Miranda admitted.

"Yeah, sorry, April," said Heidi.

"That's too bad," April said, "'cause at the end of the party, I'm giving out a grand prize for the best gag."

"What *is* the grand prize, anyway?" Sydney asked.

April pointed to a fireplace mantel near the table. On top of the mantel was a cool-looking gold trophy. It was draped with strings of pink and purple beads.

"Ta-da! There it is!" April said grandly. "And there's something inside the trophy too. It's a gift certificate for a manicure at the Pretty in Pink Salon."

"A manicure? That's awesome," said Bess. "I really hope I win!"

"I hope I win too," Katie said. "I've always wanted to go to the Pretty in Pink Salon."

Miranda stared at her nails, which were painted glittery pink. "Big deal. Heidi and I go there all the time."

"Yeah. All the time," Heidi echoed. She studied her nails too. They were painted the same shade of pink as Miranda's.

Katie frowned at Miranda and Heidi. Nancy thought she looked really annoyed. Nancy didn't blame her. Why were Miranda and Heidi acting so snotty? April was frowning at her old friends too.

After a while, April suggested that they all play games. Everyone got up from the table. First there was Hot Potato. Then Blindman's Bluff. Nancy had never played Blindman's Bluff. It was a lot of fun!

After the game, Miranda announced that she needed some lip gloss and walked over to her backpack. "Oh no!" she cried.

April turned to her. "What's up, Miranda?"

Miranda was digging through her backpack frantically. She looked upset. "My cell phone!" she exclaimed. "It's gone. Someone stole it!"

ChaPTER FiVE

A Thief on the Loose?

Heidi dropped her balloon and rushed over to Miranda. "What do you mean, someone stole your cell phone, M? That is *soooo* awful!"

"My parents are going to kill me!" Miranda cried out. "That phone cost, like, five hundred dollars or something. Or whatever that is in Japanese money."

"Japanese money is called yen," Sydney offered.

"Okay, that is so not helpful, Cindy," Miranda grumbled.

"Sydney," Sydney corrected her.

"Sydney, Cindy, whatever," said Miranda. She scanned all the faces in the room. "One of you stole my phone. Who is it? Heidi is the only one who's definitely *not* the thief, since she's my BFF."

"Thanks, M," Heidi said. She raised her hand in the air.

"You're welcome, H," Miranda replied. She and Heidi exchanged a high five.

"Maybe you lost it, Miranda," Katie suggested.

"I don't *lose* things," Miranda said huffily. "I've never lost anything in my entire life. Well, except for my MP3 player once. Or twice. And my favorite City Girls doll, too."

April looked thoughtful. "Hey! Maybe someone *pretended* to steal your phone as an April Fool's joke." She turned to the other girls. "Okay, really funny. Who did it?" she said loudly.

No one said a word.

"Come on, fess up," April persisted.

Still no one said a word.

Nancy frowned. Was April right? Was this an April Fool's joke, except that no one was fessing up?

Or was Miranda right? Was there a thief on the loose?

If there was a thief, Nancy thought, it had to be one of them. No one else had been in the basement except her, George, Bess, Katie, Sydney, Miranda, and Heidi. Of course, Mr. and Mrs. Funk had been down here too. But she couldn't imagine parents stealing a kid's cell phone!

And as far as Nancy could remember, no one had left the basement since the party started, except for Mr. and Mrs. Funk. So the phone *had* to be here somewhere.

Nancy tried to recall the last time she'd seen Miranda using her cell phone. Was it when Sydney had arrived at the party? Or sometime after that?

"When was the last time you used your phone?" Nancy asked Miranda.

Miranda scrunched up her face. "Um . . . let's see . . . it was right before we sat down to eat the kitty litter cake or whatever," she said finally. "I was talking to, um, my friend Alyssa."

"Alyssa Montoya?" Katie asked her.

"No, a different Alyssa," Miranda said quickly.

"I know!" said Nancy suddenly. "Let's just call your cell phone, Miranda. If it's in the basement somewhere, we'll hear it ringing. What does your ring tone sound like?"

"It's that supercool song 'Dancing Dogs,'" Miranda replied. "But, uh, we can't call my phone."

"Why not?" George asked her.

"Because, uh, it's on silent mode," said Miranda.

Nancy thought about this. Something didn't add up. "Hey, Miranda? Why did you put it on silent?" she asked after a moment. "I mean, it's not like we're at the movies."

"Heidi and I were, uh, at the movies last night, and I guess I forgot to turn the ringer back on," Miranda explained. "Right, H?"

Heidi hesitated, then said, "Right, M."

Nancy stared at the two girls. She had a

funny feeling that they were hiding something. Or was she just imagining things? Maybe Miranda was just acting weird because she was upset about losing her expensive cell phone.

"The cell phone's got to be down here somewhere," Bess spoke up. "Why don't we all look for it?"

"Good idea, Bess!" April told her. "Whoever finds it gets to take the rest of the kitty litter cake home," she joked.

"Ha-ha, very funny, April," said Heidi.

The eight girls split up and started combing the basement for the missing cell phone. Nancy looked under the couch. She looked under the table. She looked under the eight red folding chairs. She looked under the snack plates and even the napkins. But the cell phone was nowhere to be found.

"Any luck, Nancy?" Bess called out. She was looking under some pillows.

Nancy shook her head. "What about you?"

"Nothing. How about you, George?" Bess said.

George was looking all around a big plasma-screen TV. "I found an empty potato chip bag, two little race cars, and a toy mouse. But no cell phone," she said.

"Hey, everybody! I found it!" Sydney announced gleefully. She stood up, holding a dusty cell phone.

Miranda rolled her eyes. "That's a *green* cell

phone, dummy. I would *never* get a green cell phone."

Sydney studied the cell phone more closely. "Oh. Sorry." She flicked the phone open. "Oh. I *am* a dummy. It's not even real. It's a toy cell phone."

"That must belong to one of my—," April began.

"Okay, what's going on?" Heidi burst out, interrupting April. "This is *soooo* not funny anymore!"

Nancy glanced over at Heidi. Heidi was rooting through her backpack, which was white with pink and red hearts on it. She looked upset.

"What are you talking about, H? What's the matter?" Miranda asked her.

"My Gamer Girl console. It's gone!" Heidi cried out.

ChaPTER Six

The Red Clue

Miranda gasped. "What do you mean, your Gamer Girl is missing, H?"

Heidi was sitting on the floor and taking everything out of her backpack one by one: a pink comb, a pink brush, a pot of pink lip gloss, a pink MP3 player, a pair of pink headphones, a couple of books, and a couple of teen fashion magazines. "It's not here. It's definitely not here," she moaned. "My parents are *soooo* going to ground me forever if I don't find it!"

"When was the last time you saw it, Heidi?" Nancy asked her.

"I was playing with it . . . let's see . . . I think it was right after Sadie showed up," said Heidi.

"Sydney," Sydney corrected her.

Heidi shrugged. "Whatever. Anyway, I put it in the front pocket of my backpack. And now it's gone!"

April scanned the faces of all her friends. "Okay, is this another April Fool's joke? Fess up, people!" she demanded.

No one said a word.

"I don't think it's an April Fool's joke, April," Sydney said gravely. "I think Heidi's Gamer Girl was stolen—and Miranda's cell phone, too. In my opinion, you have a dangerous criminal on the loose!"

"I still think Miranda just lost her cell phone. And maybe you lost your Gamer Girl, too, Heidi," Katie suggested.

"No way," said Heidi. "I definitely put my Gamer Girl in the front pocket of my backpack."

"And I definitely put my cell phone in the front pocket of *my* backpack," Miranda added.

"Which means that someone took them *out* of our backpacks," Heidi concluded.

Nancy frowned. Now that *two* valuable items were missing, she had to agree with Miranda and Heidi—and Sydney, too. There had to be a thief on the loose.

The question was who.

April came up to Nancy, George, and Bess and pulled them into a quiet corner. "Listen," she said in a low voice. "I need to make sure that Miranda and Heidi find their stuff. It's my party, so I feel kind of responsible."

"That makes sense," said Nancy.

"Aren't you guys in a club that solves mysteries? Do you think you could solve *this* mystery?" April pleaded.

Nancy glanced at George and Bess. They both nodded.

Nancy turned to April. "Our club is called the Clue Crew," she said. "And we'll get on the case right away."

April beamed. "Great! So what can I do to help?"

Nancy thought for a moment. "First of all, don't tell the other girls about us working on the case yet. Second, I want you to get them out of the basement. Tell them . . . um, let's see . . . tell them you want to look for the cell phone and Gamer Girl in all the upstairs rooms."

April nodded. "Sure. What's the plan?"

"Once everyone's gone, George, Bess, and I

will go through the basement again to look for clues," Nancy told her.

"I found another empty potato chip bag," George spoke up.

"And I found another kitty toy," added Bess.

Nancy, George, and Bess were combing every inch of the basement for clues. April had managed to get the other girls upstairs, explaining that Nancy, George, and Bess were staying behind to "guard everyone's backpacks."

So far, they had not had any luck. But Nancy was convinced that there had to be a clue or two somewhere. Unless the thief was very careful, she had to have left a trace, like a loose thread from an outfit or a strand of hair.

Nancy was going over the backpacks a second time. Heidi's was white with pink and red hearts all over it. Miranda's backpack was almost identical, except that it had a small stuffed pink teddy bear attached to the strap.

Then Nancy noticed something on the front

pocket of Heidi's backpack . . . something red and very faint. She had noticed it before but had simply thought it was part of the pink and red heart design. But looking at it a second time, she realized that it definitely was not.

Nancy studied the red mark more closely. It looked like a red fingerprint!

On an impulse she grabbed Miranda's backpack, which was sitting right next to Heidi's. She scanned every inch of it carefully.

She almost cried out with excitement. There was another red mark on the front pocket, similar to the one on Heidi's backpack. It was a red fingerprint too!

"Hey!" Nancy called to her friends. "Over here!"

George and Bess hurried over. They bent their heads close to Nancy's.

"What is it, Nancy?" George asked her.

Nancy pointed the red marks out to George and Bess. "I think we have a clue," she said eagerly. "*Two* clues! They're both fingerprints."

"Good job, Nancy!" Bess praised her.

"This means that our thief has red hands!" said George. "Maybe she got red paint or red marker on them. Or something like that." She added, "Now all we have to do is check everyone's hands to see whose are red."

"I think we should check Sydney's hands first," Bess suggested. "I think she's the thief. She was really mad about not being invited to the party, remember? Maybe she crashed it so she could cause trouble."

"You're right, Bess. We should add Sydney to our suspect list," Nancy said. "Plus, what about Miranda and Heidi?"

"Huh?" said George and Bess at the same time.

"Maybe they pretended to steal their own stuff as an April Fool's joke or something," Nancy explained.

"Except they did seem pretty upset," Bess mused.

"Maybe they were just pretending," George pointed out.

Just then Nancy heard a noise. It sounded like a sneeze. She peered around the basement. The sound had come from behind the couch.

Nancy gulped. There was someone else in the room!

CHAPTER SEVEN

Sydney's Backpack

Nancy placed a finger on her lips. "Shh," she whispered to her friends.

George and Bess nodded. They looked nervous—and scared. They had heard the sneeze too.

Nancy was not happy that there was someone else in the basement. Whoever it was must have eavesdropped on the Clue Crew's entire conversation!

Nancy tiptoed over to the couch. George and Bess followed close behind. Nancy took a deep breath and peeked behind the couch.

"Hey!" someone shouted.

"Hey!" another person shouted at exactly the same time.

Nancy squinted to see in the dark space behind the couch. Two small figures were crouched there. They looked too small to be any of the other girls.

"Come on out," Nancy said. "You were spying on us, weren't you?"

There was another sneeze, and then some shuffling sounds. A moment later two small boys appeared from behind the couch. They looked like twins, with identical freckled faces,

bright blue eyes, and curly red hair that looked overdue for haircuts. Nancy guessed that they were five or six years old.

The first boy glared at the three girls. "What do you want?"

"You're not going to tell Mom and Dad, are you?" the second boy said.

"Are you April's brothers?" Bess asked them. "You look just like her."

"We do *not* look like her," the first boy protested. "April's ugly!"

"Super ugly!" the second boy agreed.

"That's not very nice," George scolded them. "What are your names?"

"Luke," mumbled the first boy.

"Liam," the second boy mumbled at the same time.

"How long have you been listening to us?" Nancy asked.

"We, uh, snuck down about five minutes ago," Luke said.

Liam nodded. "Yeah. You guys didn't notice

52

us. We're really, really good at being invisible—like Stealth Shadow."

"Fogman's more invisible, plus he has X-ray vision," Luke pointed out to his brother.

"Hmm, maybe," said Liam.

Luke turned to Nancy and her friends. He made a face, as if he were trying to look mean and scary. "Me and Liam caught you guys. You were going through everyone's backpacks. You're going to be in big trouble!"

George held up her hand. "Wait a second. We weren't going through anyone's backpacks. We were looking on the outside of Miranda's and Heidi's backpacks for clues."

"Clues? What do you mean, clues?" Liam said curiously.

Nancy explained to the two boys about the missing cell phone and Gamer Girl console. She also told them about the Clue Crew but said it was a secret. Luke's and Liam's eyes grew huge.

"You mean, you guys are detectives?" Luke said eagerly. "Like Dirk Danger, Private Eye?"

"Can we be detectives too?" Liam added.

Luke began jumping up and down. "Yay, we're going to be detectives!" he crowed.

"Um, the Clue Crew doesn't need any new members right now," Nancy said gently. She didn't want to hurt the boys' feelings. "But thanks anyway."

Liam pouted. "That's not fair! Why do you get to be part of the Clue Caboose, and we don't?"

"It's the Clue *Cruise,* dummy," Luke told his brother.

"Whatever. It's still not fair!" Liam protested.

Luke nodded. "Yeah. It's not fair!"

"So did you find any clues?" April whispered.

Nancy, George, and Bess had left the basement and found the other girls in April's room hanging out and eating popcorn. They were also talking about the missing cell phone and Gamer Girl, which nobody had found.

Nancy was about to reply when she was interrupted by Miranda. "Hey, what are you guys whispering about?" she called out.

"Aren't you three supposed to be guarding our backpacks or something?" added Heidi.

"Uh, we'll go back down in a second," Bess said quickly. "We just wanted to, uh, say hi."

George waved. "Yeah. Hi!"

"Do you guys want some popcorn?" Katie offered. She held out a big red bowl. A delicious melted-butter smell wafted from the bowl.

Nancy, George, and Bess said yes and took some of the popcorn. Then Nancy noticed something strange.

Sydney was sitting next to Katie. And she had her backpack, the blue one with dolphin stickers, on her lap. Sydney was holding on to it tightly, as though she didn't want to let it go.

Nancy smiled at Sydney. "Why do you have your backpack with you?" she asked casually.

Sydney glanced at Nancy sharply. Nancy wasn't sure, but she thought she saw a suspicious look in the other girl's eyes. "Um . . . because . . . um . . . I always carry my backpack with me

wherever I go," Sydney said after a moment.

"You do?" Nancy said.

Sydney pushed her glasses up on her nose and nodded. "Besides, there's a thief on the loose! I wouldn't want the person to steal my valuable belongings!"

"*What* valuable belongings?" Miranda asked her. "Your homework? Your pencils?" She and Heidi cracked up.

"None of your business," Sydney snapped. She stood up abruptly. "I'm going to the kitchen to get some juice," she announced, and left the room.

Bess moved closer to Nancy and George. "Why is Sydney acting so weird about her backpack?" she whispered.

"I don't know. Maybe she's hiding something in it," Nancy whispered back.

George's eyes lit up. "Like Miranda's cell phone and Heidi's Gamer Girl?"

Nancy nodded. "Exactly. Now we just have to find a way to get inside it."

Nancy, George, and Bess spent the next few minutes trying to check out everyone's hands for red marks—anything that would explain the red fingerprints on Miranda's and Heidi's backpacks. But it was hard to see people's hands. And there was no way they could just say, "Hey, could you show us your hands for a second?"

A short while later Mr. Funk popped his head through the doorway. "Hey, girls! Back to the basement. It's time for pizza and a movie," he announced.

"Yay!" all the girls cheered.

Everyone got up at once and headed downstairs. Sydney was already in the basement. She was sitting on the couch with her backpack on her lap, drinking apple juice. "Your parents told me to come down for the movie," she said to April.

Luke and Liam were there too, sitting cross-legged on the floor and playing with the little race cars that George had found. The two boys glared at Nancy, George, and Bess. Nancy guessed that they were still mad about not being able to join the Clue Crew.

Luke glanced up at his father. "We get to watch the movie too, right, Daddy?" he said.

"Yeah, Daddy!" Liam piped up.

April shook her head. "No way! This party is for big kids only."

"Oh, let them stay, April," Mr. Funk told her. "It's just a movie. They won't bother you."

Luke and Liam smiled triumphantly at April.

"Oh, all right," April grumbled. "I *guess*."

"That's the spirit," said Mr. Funk.

He walked over to the table. There were three big white pizza boxes on it, as well as a stack of fresh paper plates and napkins. "Help yourselves to the pizza, girls," he said. "And the movie's already in the DVD player. Have fun!"

"Thanks, Mr. Funk!" everyone chimed in unison.

He went upstairs. April started to turn on the DVD player.

Then she let out a shriek.

"What's wrong, April?" Nancy asked her worriedly.

April pointed to the mantel. "The trophy is gone!" she cried out.

ChaPTER EighT

One Mystery Solved

Nancy glanced quickly at the mantel. April was right. The gold trophy with the pink and purple beads was missing from its spot.

April rushed over to the mantel. There was a red folding chair in front of it. She shoved it aside so she could get a closer look. Then she sighed in frustration.

"It's totally gone!" April moaned. "The thief stole the trophy! And the gift certificate for the manicure, too!"

April turned to the others in the room. She put her hands on her hips. "Okay, who did it?" she said angrily. "You'd better tell once and for all! This is so not funny anymore!"

No one spoke—except for Luke. "When is the movie starting?" he demanded.

"I'm hungry," Liam piped up. "Can you get me some pizza, April?"

"Ask Mom or Dad. I'm busy!" April snapped.

"Sorry about your trophy, April," said Miranda sympathetically.

"Yeah, April," Heidi said. "If we figure out who stole it, maybe we can find our stuff too."

"Which are *way* more valuable than your trophy," Miranda added.

"Way," Heidi agreed.

Katie frowned at Miranda and Heidi. "That's not very nice," she said. "You guys are acting really weird today."

Nancy went up to the mantel and stood next to April. "Do you remember the last time you absolutely, positively, definitely saw the trophy?" she whispered. She didn't want anyone else in the room to hear her, in case one of them was the thief—which was probably the case.

April nodded. "It was right before we all went upstairs," she replied, also whispering. "I remember, because I was looking at it and wondering who I should give it to."

As April talked, Nancy scanned the mantel for clues. In particular she wanted to see if there might be a red fingerprint or two. But there were no fingerprints on the mantel, red or otherwise. And there were no other clues either.

"Let me go talk to George and Bess," Nancy said after a moment. "Why don't you go ahead and start the movie? That way the Clue Crew can talk about the case in private."

April nodded. "No problem. Just promise me you'll find the thief, okay?"

"I promise," Nancy told her.

But deep down, Nancy wasn't sure. This thief was proving to be trickier than she'd expected.

Nancy, George, and Bess sat on the floor in a quiet corner of the basement, discussing the case in low voices. Across the room, April, Miranda, Heidi, Katie, Sydney, Luke, and Liam were gathered in front of the TV, watching a comedy about some cute little bunny rabbits that were really evil robots. April had turned the lights down low so that the basement was dimly lit. They were all chowing down on pizza.

The twin boys kept glancing over their shoulders in the direction of Nancy and her friends.

Nancy wondered if they were still mad about not being part of the Clue Crew.

"So now there are three things missing: Miranda's cell phone, Heidi's Gamer Girl, and April's trophy and gift certificate," Nancy whispered.

"Hey! Katie really wanted that gift certificate to Pretty in Pink, remember?" Bess reminded her friends. "Maybe *she's* the thief."

"You really wanted it too, Bess," George pointed out. "Maybe *you're* the thief," she added, teasing.

Bess made a face. "Ha-ha, very funny."

"Seriously, though," George went on. "Maybe Katie stole the trophy to get the gift certificate. And maybe she stole the cell phone and Gamer Girl first—even though she didn't really want that stuff—just to confuse everyone."

Nancy considered this. "The timing doesn't work, though. There's no way Katie could have snuck down here and stolen the trophy. The three of us were here looking for clues, remember? And Katie was in April's room the whole time we were here."

Bess and George both nodded in agreement.

Then Nancy's eyes lit up. "But someone else *did* have a chance to sneak down here and steal it. She left April's room before the rest of us, to get some juice."

"Sydney!" George said loudly, forgetting to whisper.

Nancy put her fingers to her lips. "Shh!"

But it was too late. Sydney had overheard.

She stood up from her spot in front of the TV and came marching over to the three girls. Her blue backpack with the dolphins was slung across her shoulders.

Sydney folded her arms across her chest. "I heard my name. You three are obviously discussing me. What's going on?"

Nancy tried frantically to think of a white lie that would explain why they were talking about Sydney. But before she could speak, Bess jumped to her feet.

"We've figured it all out. You're the thief! You're hiding Miranda's cell phone, Heidi's Gamer Girl, and April's trophy in your backpack!" Bess blurted out.

"Let's see your hands!" added George, also jumping to her feet.

"M-my . . . hands?" Sydney stammered. She stuck them out, then turned them faceup.

There was no sign of red on them.

"Okay, but you're still our thief," Bess insisted. "Open up your backpack right this second!"

Sydney clutched her backpack tightly. "I refuse! It's, um, private."

"It's private because it has the stuff you stole in it?" Nancy asked her.

Sydney shook her head. "No, it's private because . . . because . . ."

Sydney looked really uncomfortable. After a moment, she sighed and opened her backpack. She pulled something out of it. "Here," she said abruptly, handing the item to Nancy.

Nancy took it. It was a small package

wrapped in shiny blue paper with a curly white ribbon. "What is it?" she asked Sydney, puzzled.

Just then April came over to the four of them. "What's going on?" she whispered to Nancy and the others.

Sydney took the gift-wrapped package from Nancy and handed it to April. "Here," she said. "It's for you."

"A present for me?" April said, looking confused. "Why? It's not my birthday or anything."

"I got you a present to say I'm sorry," Sydney explained. "I'm sorry about the big fight we had last week. I figured that was why you didn't invite me to your party. And I'm sorry I crashed it. Nancy, George, and Bess didn't really invite me. I made up that part."

April grinned. "That's okay. I'm sorry too, Sydney. That fight was half my fault."

The two friends hugged. Nancy glanced at April and Sydney. Sydney *had* been telling the truth about being BFFs with April, after all!

April opened the present. Inside was a book called *101 Awesome Jokes*. "Excellent!" April told Sydney happily. "Thanks!"

"You're welcome," said Sydney. The two friends hugged again.

Bess sighed. "Well, now we're back to square one. Who's the thief?"

"I don't know," Nancy said.

She fell silent as she considered Bess's question. She scanned the room slowly, taking in every detail. She noted that Katie, Miranda, Heidi, and the twins were still watching the movie and eating pizza. She saw all of April's goofy party decorations. She glanced at the empty mantel where the trophy used to be. She noticed the red folding chair in front of the mantel.

Then she looked at the table with the pizza boxes on top of it and the red folding chairs around it. She counted the chairs around the table. One, two, three, four, five, six, seven . . .

Something clicked inside her brain. She smiled excitedly at April. "I know who stole the trophy!" she announced.

Chapter Nine

Bess's Discovery

"Yay, Nancy! The Clue Crew solved the mystery!" April said eagerly. "So who is it? Who's the thief?"

Nancy didn't reply. She walked over to the big plasma-screen TV, picked up the remote control, and hit the pause button.

"Hey!" Luke and Liam complained.

"Why did you stop the movie?" Miranda demanded.

"Yeah, why?" Heidi chimed in.

"It's just getting to the good part, where the evil rabbit robots decide to take over New York City," Katie added. "You guys want to watch with us?"

"Listen, everyone!" Nancy said loudly. "I have an announcement. April asked George, Bess, and me to figure out who the thief is. Right now we need everyone to go and stand by the mantel—one at a time."

Bess moved closer to Nancy. "What are you doing, Nancy?" she whispered.

"I want to see how tall everyone is," Nancy whispered back.

Miranda sighed dramatically. "This is bogus."

"Yeah, it's *soooo* bogus," Heidi agreed.

"Can everyone puh-lease just do what Nancy says?" April said. "Here, I'll go first."

April walked over to the mantel and stood in front of it. "There," she said. "Who's next?"

"I'll go," Katie offered. She walked over to the mantel and stood in front of it, next to April.

Sydney went after Katie—then Miranda, then Heidi. Nancy glanced at Luke and Liam, who were still glued to their spots in front of the TV.

"Luke and Liam—you too," Nancy said.

Luke frowned at Nancy. "We don't have to

71

listen to you. You're not the boss of us!"

"Yeah," Liam piped up.

"Do what Nancy says, or I'll tell Mom and Dad!" April scolded her brothers.

Luke made a face. *"Fine.* Come on, Liam."

The two boys stood up and marched defiantly to the mantel. Nancy realized that they were way too short to reach the top of the mantel—at least without help.

"Okay, what did you guys do with April's trophy?" Nancy asked Luke and Liam.

Luke's face flushed beet red. So did Liam's. "W-what are you t-talking about?" Luke stammered. Liam didn't say a word.

April gasped. "You guys took my trophy?" she cried out. "I am *so* telling Mom and Dad."

Luke started to say something, then clamped his mouth shut. Liam did likewise.

"This is boring. I'm going back to the movie," Miranda said.

"Me too," said Heidi.

The two girls went back to the TV and switched on the DVD player. Katie and Sydney joined them, but Nancy noticed out of the corner of her eye that Katie was watching her, George, and Bess. *What's up with that?* Nancy wondered.

April turned to Nancy. "How did you know it was Luke and Liam?"

Nancy pointed to the red folding chair near the mantel. "That chair was at the table, with the other chairs," she explained. "But someone moved it next to the mantel. I figured it was them because they had to stand on it to reach the trophy. Everyone in the room is tall enough to reach the top of the mantel—"

"Except for my shrimp-sized little brothers," April said knowingly.

"We are *not* shrimp-sized!" Luke protested.

"Maybe not. But you did steal your sister's trophy, right?" George asked them.

Bess bent down and smiled sweetly at Luke and Liam. "I don't know about everyone else. But I think it's supercool that you pulled off such a major crime."

Liam's face lit up. "You do?"

Bess nodded. "Definitely! It's like something the Maniac would do."

"Or the Bandit," Luke agreed.

"So why did you guys do it?" Bess asked them.

Luke stared down at the ground. "W-well . . . we didn't like it when you wouldn't let us join your Clue Cruise," he said in a quiet voice.

"Yeah. It wasn't fair," Liam added.

Nancy considered this. "I'm sorry about that," she said. "So . . . did you take Miranda's cell phone and Heidi's Gamer Girl, too?"

Luke's head shot up. "No way!"

"We didn't take those things," said Liam.

Nancy studied the two boys. They seemed to

be telling the truth. That meant that there was still another thief on the loose!

"So where did you hide the trophy?" Bess asked the boys.

In response, Luke took Bess's hand and led her to a stack of cardboard boxes in the corner of the basement. Liam trailed after them. Luke pulled the trophy out from behind the stack. The trophy was dusty but intact.

"You hid my trophy back there in that dirty, yucky corner?" April said to her brothers. "Thanks a lot!"

"I'll clean it off for you, April," Bess offered quickly. "I have to wash my hands, too. They're totally covered with dust now!"

Bess disappeared into the bathroom. April turned to Nancy. "Thanks for finding my trophy and gift certificate," she said gratefully.

Nancy smiled. "No problem. Now we just have to find the *other* thief."

"Do you know who it could be?" said April.

Just then Bess came running out of the bath-

room, trophy in hand. She had a big smile on
her face.

"Nancy! George! April!" Bess said breath-
lessly. "I think I just solved the rest of the
mystery!"

ChaPTER TEN

The Best Gag of All

"What do you mean, you've solved the rest of the mystery?" Nancy asked Bess.

"I thought you went to the bathroom to wash your hands," George added, confused.

Bess nodded. "I did. See?"

She turned her hands palms up. Nancy saw immediately that they were splotched with red. It was the same shade of red as the fingerprints on Miranda's and Heidi's backpacks!

"I washed my hands in the bathroom with the bar of soap that was there," Bess said. "The soap was white, but it turned my hands red."

Nancy turned to April. "Does your family use some kind of magic soap, or what?"

"I bought that soap at Gagtime," April replied. "I put it in the bathroom for the party, as a joke."

"I saw that soap when we were at Gagtime!" George recalled.

Nancy remembered seeing that soap too. Her heart was pounding with excitement. She couldn't believe it. Bess had figured out a major piece of the puzzle!

"Our thief must have washed her hands with the soap, then left the red fingerprints on Miranda's and Heidi's backpacks," Nancy said out loud.

"Red fingerprints? What red fingerprints?" April said, puzzled.

"I'll explain later," said Nancy. "I think I know how to find our thief."

Without another word, she hurried over to Miranda, Heidi, Katie, and Sydney. They had all taken a break from the movie to get more pizza. The DVD was on pause. The twins had gone upstairs.

"Hey, Nancy. Do you want pepperoni or plain?" Katie asked her.

Nancy shook her head. "No thanks, Katie. I just wanted to tell everyone that April has the coolest soap in the bathroom. You should all check it out!"

Miranda's face lit up. "Really? Is it from Pretty in Pink?" She started heading for the bathroom.

"Is it Mango Madness or Fresh 'n Fruity?" Heidi asked. She followed Miranda.

"Could I go first? I got tomato sauce all over my hands," Sydney said, trailing after them. "Is the soap really perfumey, Nancy? I don't like really perfumey soap."

Katie was the only one to hold back. "Not me! That soap is weird," she complained.

Miranda, Heidi, and Sydney stopped in

their tracks. "What do you mean, it's weird?" Miranda demanded.

"When did you use it, Katie?" Nancy asked her casually.

Katie made a face. "I washed my hands with it while we were having snacks. But it's some kind of practical-joke soap. It turned my hands red! I think I got most of the red off, but"—she glanced at her hands—"not all of it. I still have three red fingers. Yuck!"

Nancy, George, Bess, and April glanced knowingly at one another. They had found their thief!

"What?" Katie frowned at the four girls. "Why are you all looking at each other like that?"

"We found red fingerprints on Miranda's and Heidi's backpacks—," Nancy began.

"Which means that you're the thief," April finished. "Why, Katie? Did you want to ruin my party, or what?"

Katie's eyes grew huge. Her lower lip trembled. "I'm really, really sorry, April," she said after a moment. "I didn't mean for it to go this far. And

I didn't mean to ruin your party or anything."

"*You* took our stuff, Katie?" Miranda said, shocked.

"That is *soooo* lame, Katie," added Heidi. "Give it back—like, now!"

Katie turned to gaze at Miranda and Heidi. "I stole your stuff because I was tired of hearing you bragging about it," she said, sounding upset. "I was going to give it back right away and act like it was an April Fool's joke or whatever. But you kept acting so mean to everybody. I decided I wouldn't give it back until you started being nice again."

"Nice . . . *again*?" Bess repeated, confused. "I don't get it."

"You guys are usually really nice in school," Katie told Miranda and Heidi. "But for some reason, today you started acting like snobby rich girls or something. It was totally weird."

April nodded. "I kind of noticed that too. But that doesn't make it cool for you to steal their stuff, Katie."

"I know," Katie agreed. "I shouldn't have done it."

Katie walked over to her backpack, opened a zipped compartment in the back, and pulled out Miranda's My-Fone and Heidi's Gamer Girl. "Here you go," she said, handing the items over to the two girls. "I'm sorry. April's right. I shouldn't have stolen your stuff."

"Hmm. Should we accept her apology, H?" Miranda asked Heidi.

"I don't know, M. Should we?" Heidi replied.

The two girls exchanged a mysterious smile. Then Miranda pushed a button on her cell phone. It squirted water at Katie!

Katie shrieked as the water sprayed her face. "W-what's th-that?" she sputtered.

Heidi pushed a button on her Gamer Girl. It squirted water too. Katie shrieked again.

Miranda and Heidi started cracking up. "April Fool's!" they said at the same time.

Nancy couldn't believe it. The pricey, impossible-to-get "My-Fone from Japan" and

the "Gamer Girl from Sweden" were fakes—just like George's squirting calculator!

"You told us to bring gags to the party, right?" Miranda said to April, still cracking up. "So we bought the phone and the gaming console at a gag store in Chicago. We decided to act like snobby rich girls for the day and show off our expensive new 'gear.' That was our gag. We fooled you, didn't we?"

"You sure did," April said. She looked stunned.

"When someone stole our stuff, we decided to keep the gag going and act super upset," Heidi went on.

"You guys are such good actors," Bess told them.

Miranda flipped her blond hair over her shoulders. "Thanks! Hollywood, here we come."

April grinned at Miranda and Heidi. "You had us all totally fooled. That means only one thing."

"What?" asked Heidi.

April took the trophy from Bess, who was still holding it, and held it out to Miranda and Heidi. "Ta-da! You guys win the grand prize for the best gag!" she announced.

There was clapping and cheering all around. Miranda whispered something in Heidi's ear. Heidi nodded.

"Just to show there's no hard feelings," Miranda said, "this is for you, Katie."

Miranda reached into the trophy and pulled

out the gift certificate for the Pretty in Pink Salon. She handed it to Katie.

Katie smiled happily. "You guys are the best. Thanks! And again, I'm so sorry about what I did." She reached over and hugged Miranda and Heidi.

George leaned over to Nancy and Bess. "Wow. Was this one of our trickiest mysteries to solve, or what?" she said.

Nancy grinned. "It was. And that's no April Fool's joke!"

Fool Your Friends with Nancy's Delicious "Dirt" Cake!

Have some April Fool's fun by serving your friends "dirt" cake. It *looks* like a pail full of dirt and bugs. Gross! But it's really a tasty, easy-to-make treat made of chocolate cookies, whipped cream, and other yummy (and edible!) ingredients.

You Will Need:

2 packages of instant chocolate or vanilla
   pudding mix (usually 3 to 4 oz. each)
1 cup of powdered sugar
1 8-oz. package of cream cheese (leave it
   out of the fridge for an hour, to soften)
1 8-oz. container of frozen whipped cream
   topping (thawed)
1-pound package of cream-filled chocolate
   cookies
A clean (toy) sand pail

A clean (toy) plastic shovel

Some gummy worms (optional)

Some plastic spiders and other plastic bugs
(optional)

A plastic flower (optional)

Get ready to make some dirt!

❀ Combine pudding mix, powdered sugar, and cream cheese in a bowl.

❀ In another bowl, crush the cream-filled cookies so you get a bunch of little chunks and crumbs that look like dirt. You can also use a food processor, with a parent's help. Pour the cookie bits into the container of whipped cream topping and mix together.

❀ Using a spoon, put a layer of the cookies and whipped cream mixture into the pail. Then add a layer of the pudding mix/powdered sugar/cream cheese mixture. Keep doing this, alternating layers and ending with the cookies and whipped cream mixture on top. You can also add gummy worms as you go along.

❀ If you have them, add some plastic bugs, a plastic flower, and more gummy worms on top. Stick the plastic shovel into the "dirt" and serve.

BON APPÉTIT!